Across the Oregon Trail

Written by Susan Brocker
Illustrated by Robert Quimby

Between the laughing and the crying,
The living and the dying,
The singing and the sighing,
The wheels roll west.

                                    Trail Song

CONTENTS

Introduction	New Frontiers	4
Map	The Oregon Trail	6
Chapter One	The Runaway Wagon	8
Chapter Two	Lightning Ride	17
Chapter Three	Lost on the Prairie	26
Chapter Four	The Buffalo Hunt	35
Chapter Five	Fort Laramie	40
Chapter Six	Hold Your Fire!	46
Chapter Seven	The River Crossing	51
Chapter Eight	Across the Desert	56
Chapter Nine	The Fall	66
Chapter Ten	Into the Mountains	71
Chapter Eleven	The Short Cut	79
Chapter Twelve	The Rock of the Bear	87
Chapter Thirteen	The Way Home	95
Chapter Fourteen	Journey's End	99

INTRODUCTION
NEW FRONTIERS

Although this is a work of fiction, much of the detail it contains is based on fact. From the 1840s to the 1870s, up to half a million people crossed the Oregon Trail. Families packed their possessions into covered wagons pulled by oxen teams, left their homes and everything they knew on the east coast of North America, and set off overland on a long and dangerous trek to Oregon on the west coast.

They went in search of a better life, lured by stories of a rich and beautiful land. Many of the travellers were poor and landless, and had dreams of starting up their own farms.

The 3,490-kilometre journey across the Oregon Trail took, on average, six months to complete. The pioneers travelled through a wild and untamed land of wide prairies, vast deserts, and steep mountains. Heading into new frontiers held countless dangers. There were many deaths along the way from disease and accidents. Often, women were forced to continue the journey without their husbands, children without their parents.

Many of the pioneers who made the long journey across the Oregon Trail kept diaries of their experiences. A lot of the things that Jem encounters in this story are based upon these true accounts.

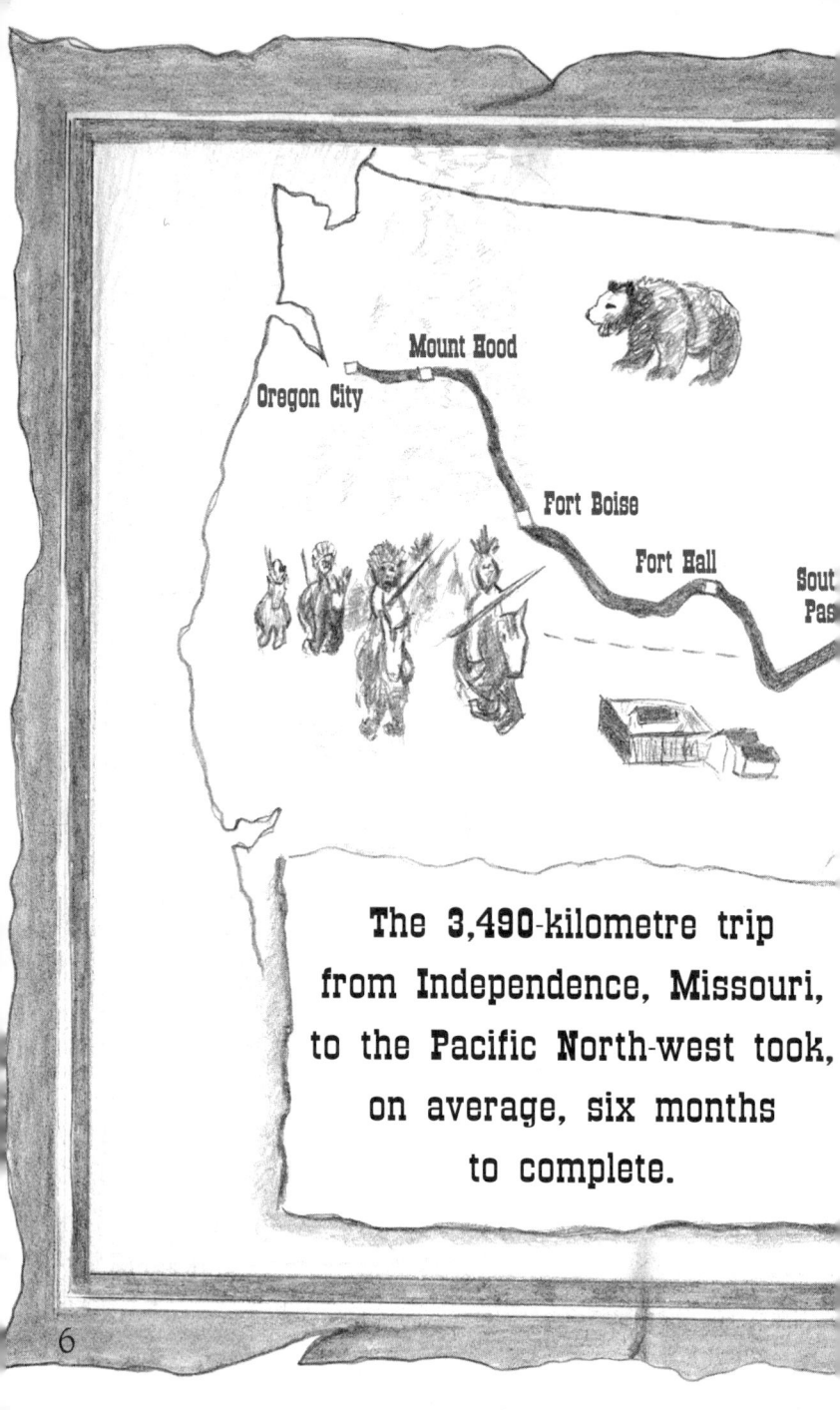

The 3,490-kilometre trip from Independence, Missouri, to the Pacific North-west took, on average, six months to complete.

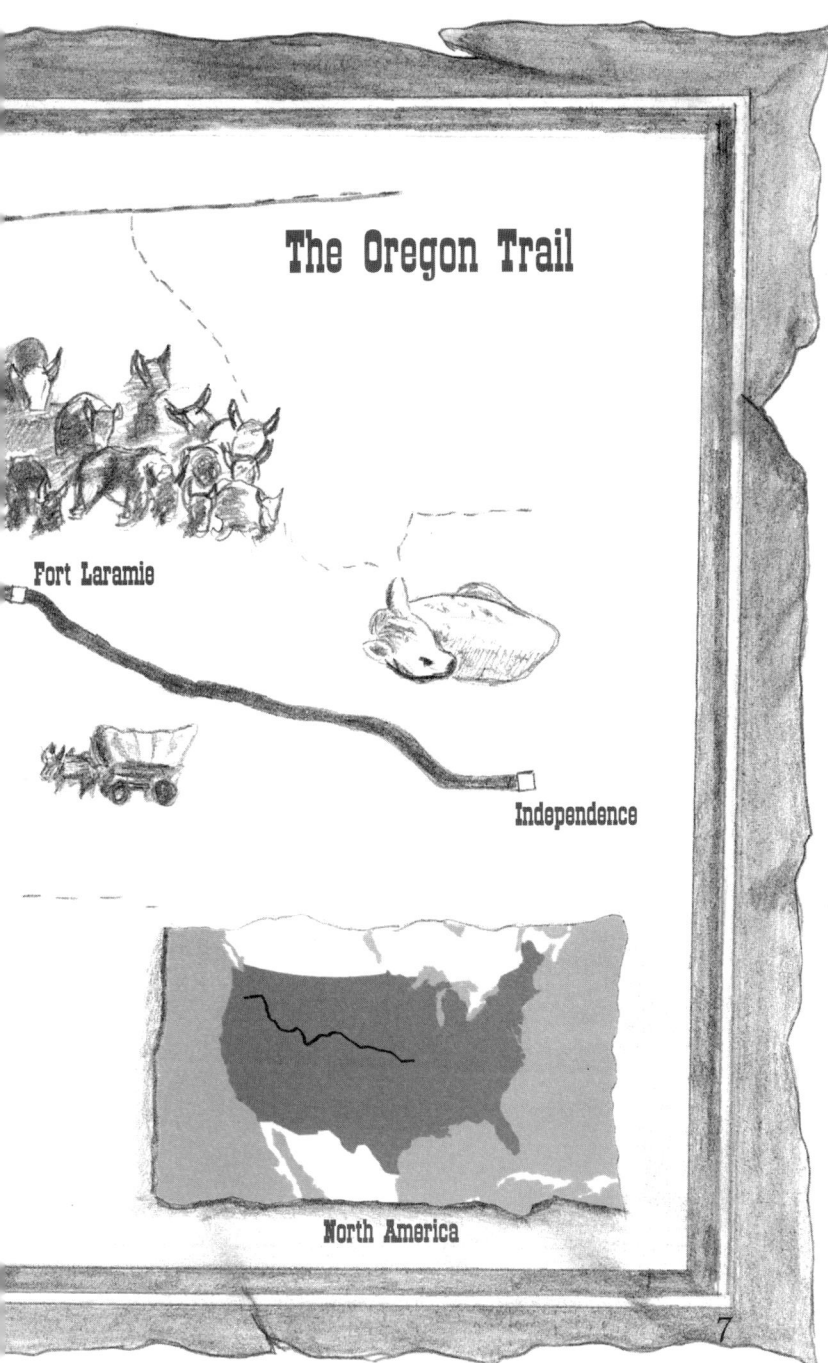

CHAPTER ONE
THE RUNAWAY WAGON

He could feel the bear's hot breath upon his face. His heart thumped so loudly he was sure it would leap out of his chest.

"Please, please, leave me alone," prayed Jem. But the grizzly kept on coming. Jem lay curled up tightly, his arms wrapped around his head. The bear pushed at Jem with its snout, trying to roll him over. Jem could smell its foul breath and even see one red, angry eye. Then the bear let out a roar that shattered the night. Jem screamed.

"Wake up, Jem. Wake up," called his mother. "You're having another nightmare."

Jem woke to the pitch-black darkness of the tent. His mother was gently shaking him, and his sister was muttering sleepily, "Can't you shut him up, Ma?"

The Runaway Wagon

"It's time to get up anyway. The fire has to be lit and the tent packed up," Ma said. The baby started to cry in the darkness as Jem rummaged for his clothes. Outside the tent, the rest of the wagon train was stirring. Fires glimmered and dark shapes huddled in the cold. Wagons encircled the camp, their cotton canopies glowing ghostly white.

"Get up the cattle! Get up the cattle!" yelled the trail captain. He rode through the group of campers on his black mare, spurring the men into action. His rifle rested against the high pommel of his saddle, and a bullet pouch and powder horn hung by his side.

Jem hated this time of day more than any other. Out there in the dark, Goliath was waiting for him. He wondered what he had planned for him today.

Along with the other oxen, Goliath was left free to graze outside the corral overnight. Guards made sure the cattle didn't stray too far, but Jem knew that Goliath would be as far away as possible.

Jem trudged out onto the plains carrying a long stock whip. The first rays of light were creeping across the prairie, and he could just make out the bulky forms of the oxen. The captain and some other men cantered past on horseback. They would round up the group and bring them all in. All, that is, except for Goliath. It was a game he played. "Catch me if you can, Jem," he seemed to say.

At last, Jem saw the big ox grazing on his own behind a clump of spindly sagebrush. He approached him from behind and prodded him with the butt of the whip. Goliath kept on munching. Jem prodded him again. Goliath still kept on munching.

"You'll never move him like that," yelled the captain from his horse. "Yaa, yaa, move on out," he bellowed at Goliath. Goliath gave him a baleful look and set off for camp at a trot. Jem had to run to keep up.

The rest of the oxen were gathered into the corral of circled wagons. Jem's sister, Ella, had caught the rest of the team and tethered them

The Runaway Wagon

to the wagon. "What took you so long?" she called out.

Ma was bent over the campfire cooking breakfast. The buffalo chips she had collected for fuel were damp, and black smoke swirled about her face. Ella began to load up the wagon. It was filled with tools, spare wagon parts, small pieces of furniture, pots and pans, clothes, bedding, food for the stock, and food for themselves. Everything they owned had to fit into a tiny space no more than one metre wide by four metres long.

Jem turned to the task of yoking up the team. As he approached Goliath nervously, the animal swung his massive head around to look at him, his hooked horns held high. "Look only at his eyes," Jem told himself. At least they looked gentle and kind.

Jem struggled to lift the heavy wooden yokes onto the backs of the oxen. He fumbled with the collars and tangled up the traces. The oxen stamped their feet impatiently. Suddenly, the captain fired a rifle shot into the air and yelled, "Move 'em out!" The lead oxen and wagons broke off from the circle, and the rest of the train followed slowly like a huge snake unfurling from its sleep. A long line of over sixty wagons soon made its bumpy way along the plains with a straggle of men, women, children, dogs, horses, cattle, and sheep following alongside.

The prairie echoed with the sound of stock whips cracking, men yelling to their oxen, and cattle bellowing. Teams jockeyed for position, oxen pushed and shoved, and wagons bumped into each other. The captain galloped along the line, yelling commands at those who were less experienced at keeping their teams under control.

Jem could sense that Goliath and the team were restless. They were already ignoring his commands. When he called "haw" to turn left, they pulled right. When he called "gee" to turn right, they turned left. It didn't help when the captain yelled at him, "Boy, you're driving those cattle on the wrong side!"

The Runaway Wagon

"Greenhorn," jeered the Murphy boys, who were driving their father's team just in front of him. "Go back to the city where you belong!"

Jem fought to keep Goliath under control. He could feel the huge beast pulling away. Ma and Ella were calling out to him to slow down. If only he could! The wagon was starting to grumble and groan as the wheels bounced over the rough terrain. "Whoa, whoa!" he cried. The team lumbered on.

"Pull those cattle up, boy," called the captain. Jem didn't have the strength. He tried to keep alongside the team, but the massive wagon wheels rolled closer and closer, until he was sure they would roll right over him. In a blind panic, he leaped to the side, and the oxen and wagon charged on ahead of him.

The oxen raced out of control. The side of the wagon smashed against the tailgate of the wagon in front, and pots and pans, food and clothes were thrown onto the ground.

"Go after them, Jem!" screamed Ella. Jem could barely clamber up off the ground. The wagon slammed over a rock, teetered on one wheel, and nearly tipped. Goliath and the team galloped on, dragging the wobbling wagon behind them.

The captain rode his horse alongside Goliath and reached down for the traces. He managed to grab them, but Jem hadn't properly fixed them to the yoke. The traces came free.

"Runaways! Watch out ahead!" cried the captain. In that moment, Jem could see all his family's dreams shattered. If the wagon smashed, everything they had hoped for would be lost and they could not go on.

Suddenly, Jem saw a spotted horse and its young rider galloping up from the back of the wagon line. They drew up alongside the oxen, and the boy spurred his horse on. Then he leaped into the air and landed on the back of Goliath. Reaching over the yoke, he grabbed Goliath's halter, pulling it to the right and calling out to the oxen. The great beasts began to slow. Eventually, they drew to a

The Runaway Wagon

stop, their sides heaving and froth dripping from their mouths.

"Thank you, Little Bear," called the captain. "You've saved us from a stampede." Cantering up, the captain told Jem in a low voice, "If you can't get this team of yours under control, you and your folks are out of this train."

Little Bear stood quietly, patting the oxen. Once they were calm, he fixed the traces properly and handed the reins to Jem. Jem couldn't even bring himself to say thank you. The boy was the son of the Native American guide, and Jem had always thought how confident and sure he looked. Now Jem felt like an idiot standing there in front of him covered with dirt.

"Had to get help from Little Bear, eh kid?" called Billy, the oldest of the Murphy boys.

Ma and Ella caught up, carrying baby Matthew and some items that had fallen from the wagon. Before Jem could speak, Ma smiled and said, "The wagon's in one piece. It could have been worse."

15

Jem couldn't bear to look at her. He tried to move the team, but Goliath wouldn't budge.

"Can't you do anything?" groaned Ella.

Little Bear gently took the reins from Jem and moved behind the oxen. "Move on," he said, clucking his tongue. The oxen plodded forward, with the wagon creaking behind.

"You're standing too close to them with the whip," Little Bear said to Jem. "They see the whip from the corner of their eyes and it scares them. If you keep back and talk to them, they will understand what you want."

He handed the reins back to Jem, and Jem clucked softly at the oxen. They moved on, their ears twitching back and forth as they listened to Jem's words. Jem was in control for the first time.

Little Bear leaped up onto his spotted horse and cantered off. Jem still hadn't managed to say thank you.

CHAPTER TWO
LIGHTNING RIDE

Since starting on their long journey from Independence, Missouri, over a month ago, the wagon party had settled into a daily routine. They woke well before sunrise, had their breakfast of coffee, bacon, and bread, loaded up the wagons, yoked the oxen, and hit the trail. There was an hour's break for lunch, and they set up camp at about six in the evening. The wagons were pulled up in a circle, with the front of each wagon butting up against the wagon ahead to form a stockade. The tents were pitched in the middle.

Most evenings were spent singing and storytelling around the campfires. Jem enjoyed this time of day most of all. This was when he could escape. Nothing more was expected of him; all the animals had been tended to, the wagon checked, and any repairs made as best he could. Jem was free to read his book by the light of the campfire.

"Let's go and join the Murphys at their campfire, Jem," suggested his sister.

Ella wasn't allowed to leave the wagon alone, so she was forever pestering Jem to visit the other campfires with her. Usually it was to visit the Murphy family. Old Man Murphy was cantankerous, but Mrs Murphy doted on Ella. The four Murphy boys were always giving Jem a hard time. Billy Murphy was about Jem's age, although at least a head taller. He acted as if he knew it all; the trouble was that, when it came to this kind of life, he really did. He'd been brought up on a farm and knew all about animals. He was always teasing Jem about being a city boy, and all the other boys joined in the teasing, too.

"Forget it, Ella. Leave me alone."

"Why must you be so dull? Why can't you be more fun?"

"Ella, that's enough," warned Ma.

Lightning Ride

At that moment, Little Bear joined them at the campfire. For once, Jem was pleased to see him. With luck, it would take Ella's mind off the Murphys. Little Bear and Ella had become friends since the incident with the runaway oxen. Ella was crazy about horses, and she wanted to know all about Little Bear's beautiful spotted horse. Little Bear told them that his horse was called an Appaloosa.

"Have all Appaloosas got spots the way yours has?" Ella asked.

"Mostly. Some are covered with spots like my horse. Others have got only a few spots. But all Appaloosas have got eyes just like people's – you can see the whites. And a lot of them have got striped hooves," Little Bear said. Ella nicknamed Little Bear's horse Lightning, because the stripes on his hooves looked like forks of lightning.

Jem tried not to stare at Little Bear as he sat opposite the campfire chatting to Ella. He noticed that Little Bear had a necklace made of bear claws around his neck. He probably wrestled a bear to get that, Jem thought bitterly. Little Bear didn't seem afraid of anything.

"Would you like to join us for dinner, Little Bear?" Ma asked. No other mother would have invited Little Bear to eat with them, Jem knew. Most people on the wagon trail ignored Little Bear and his father, Swift Arrow.

"No thank you. I've come to ask Jem if he would like to ride with me at lunch tomorrow," said Little Bear. "He can ride Lightning, and I can ride my father's horse."

"I'm sure he'd love to," Jem's mother said, before Jem had the chance to say no. Jem wished his mother hadn't answered for him. The last thing in the world he wanted to do was ride Lightning.

That night, Jem couldn't get to sleep. He dreaded the thought of riding Lightning. What if he fell off and made a fool of himself? Jem had only ever ridden their old grey mare, Tess, and she never went faster than a walk. Lightning pranced and reared and tossed his head and could move as fast as

Lightning Ride

his name. Jem was sure he would have nightmares about it.

When Jem did fall asleep, however, it was not Lightning that he dreamed about. It was something far more frightening. The grizzly bear was back. This time, it had Jem by the neck and was shaking him like a rag doll. Jem woke up screaming once again.

U U U

At noon the next day, the captain rode down the straggling line of wagons, calling everybody to a halt for lunch. It had been a long, hot morning. Jem loosened the traces on the oxen for them to rest. It was tiring work pulling the wagons in the scorching sun. Ma and Ella were tired, too. At the start of the journey, they had ridden on the front of the wagon, but the ride was very bumpy and uncomfortable. Now they took turns walking and carrying baby Matthew or riding on Tess.

Their feet ached from traipsing across the hard, hot ground.

Jem hoped that Little Bear might have forgotten his offer of a ride, but, as soon as the wagon party had settled down to lunch, Little Bear rode up on his father's horse, leading Lightning. Lightning was wearing a wooden saddle covered with wolf skin and decorated with beadwork. Ornaments were attached to his bridle and stirrups, and a woven breast collar hung around his neck. He looked impressive.

"I thought we could ride over to that outcrop of rocks," Little Bear said, handing Lightning's reins over to Jem. Lightning danced and snorted, and Jem's stomach turned. He managed to get his foot in the rawhide stirrup, and swung up into the saddle. All the while, his stomach was doing little flips. To his surprise, he felt fine on Lightning's back. The horse's dancing step was smooth and gentle, like sitting on a boat dipping and ducking on the waves.

Lightning Ride

"Do you want to go for a canter?" Little Bear asked.

"Yes, I think so," replied Jem.

Little Bear clicked his tongue and, before Jem had a chance to wonder if he was doing the right thing, Lightning was off. Jem had never gone so fast. He leaned over the horse's neck and watched the ground disappear beneath Lightning's flashing feet. He heard himself yipping and yelling, and then they were passing Little Bear and his horse. The two boys raced towards the outcrop of rocks. Lightning's mane was flying in Jem's face and the wind was whipping through his hair. When they reached the rocks, Jem and Lightning were well out in front.

"That wasn't a canter, that was a gallop!" shouted Little Bear, laughing as he pulled his horse to a stop.

"It was flying!" Jem grinned at him and patted Lightning's neck.

The boys turned their horses back to camp. The huddle of wagons up ahead looked tiny in the vastness of the plains. It seemed to Jem that you could see forever across the rolling landscape, where the long, golden grass moved like a restless sea in the wind.

"Do you ever get tired of this flat land?" Jem asked Little Bear.

"Yes, I miss the mountains and the lakes. I would like to go home."

Jem was surprised. "You mean you don't live on the plains? Where are you from?"

"My family and I come from the mountains far away to the north-west. It's near the place you are going to. That's why my father is guiding the group. He knows the mountains very well."

Jem wanted to know more. He thought that all Native Americans lived on the plains. He knew Little Bear was Nez Perce, but he thought it might be rude to ask too many questions. Instead he said, "Lightning is a wonderful horse. He's very special."

"The Nez Perce have bred the spotted horse for many years. Only the fastest and cleverest horses are chosen. They run free in the valley where my people live."

Jem rode Lightning proudly into camp. The horse pranced and danced, and Jem sat still and deep in the saddle the way Little Bear had shown him. Billy and his brothers gawked as he rode by.

"Town boy didn't fall off the big scary horse then?" Billy Murphy called out.

Jem hoped that Ma and Ella would see him riding Lightning so confidently, but, as they rode up to the wagon, his sister and mother were far too busy fussing over a tiny fawn to notice.

CHAPTER THREE
LOST ON THE PRAIRIE

Ella was trying to feed the tiny fawn from a mug. She was spilling more on herself than down the fawn's throat.

"Where did that come from?" Jem asked as he dismounted.

"I found it in those trees over there," Ella said, pointing to a stand of cottonwoods by the camp. "It was fast asleep, all curled up in a tight ball!"

"You should return the fawn," said Little Bear. "Its mother has left it there for safe keeping while she goes out to graze. She'll be back for it soon."

"But it followed me back to camp. It's lonely. It wants to stay with me!"

"You should listen to Little Bear, Ella. The fawn will die without its mother," Ma said.

Lost on the Prairie

Ella made a face and said she would return the fawn. She wandered out of camp with the little fawn wobbling behind her on its unsteady legs.

By the time they were packed up, Ella had returned. "Move 'em out! Move 'em out!" called the captain, and the wagon train rumbled out across the plains. Jem walked behind the plodding Goliath. He no longer needed to carry a whip – they understood each other now. So most of Jem's time could be spent daydreaming. This afternoon, he thought a lot about riding Lightning. He wished his father could have seen him. He would have been proud.

The wagon train made slow progress in the hot sun. When they reached a swift-flowing stream, the captain decided they could stop early for the day to give the cattle a rest and to catch up on repairs. Some groups went down to the stream to wash their dusty clothing, and the children followed to splash around and cool off. Ella was the first to go, forgetting her chores and leaving it to Jem to collect buffalo chips for the fire.

While Ella, Ma, and Matthew were gone and the rest of the camp was quiet, Jem heard a plaintive bleating coming from the back of the wagon. He climbed onto the wagon and peered in. There in the corner, tucked up in Ella's bedroll, was the fawn. Jem was furious. Ella never listened.

Jem took Ella aside when she returned. "Ma told you to take that fawn back to its mother. Do you know what's going to happen now? It's going to die, that's what! You can't feed it. Only its mother can do that."

"It's not my fault. I tried to return it, but it followed me back. I couldn't desert it! Please don't tell Ma, Jem. You know she'd never trust me again."

Jem felt sorry for Ella. He also knew that Little Bear was right – the fawn would die without its mother. "I'll take it back while Ma's down at the stream. It won't take long on horseback."

Before his mother could return and ask him what he was up to, Jem saddled Tess and set off with the fawn nestled in the saddle pack. It was easy to retrace the wagon train's path, as the wheels had flattened the prairie grass and left ruts in the soil. At last, he reached the area where they had camped for lunch, and he made his way to the cottonwoods. He placed the bleating fawn under a tree and rode off to a safe distance. Soon a deer approached, and Jem watched happily as mother and baby were reunited.

It wasn't until the light began to fade that Jem realized he'd been away far too long. Night fell rapidly on the plains, and soon he would be unable to see the way back. He had not brought a lamp of any kind, or even any matches. Jem was terrified of spending the night out on the prairie alone, but he had left himself little choice.

The night was inky black. There wasn't even a slice of moon to light the way. Tess stumbled as they wandered aimlessly in the dark. They would have to stop and wait until morning to find the path. Jem unsaddled the mare by touch, as he couldn't see the girth or straps. Then he groped around for a heavy rock and rolled it on top of the reins to keep the horse from straying off. Finally, he lay down on the hard ground, with his head against the saddle.

It was chilly after the searing heat of the day. Jem shivered and pulled the saddle blanket around his shoulders. Close by, coyotes yapped to each other and, in the distance, wolves howled into the night. Jem thought of the graves he had seen along the trail; the graves of travellers who would never reach Oregon. Many of them had been dug up by wolves and their bones scattered across the prairie. Sometimes wolves circled their camp, although they never came too close with all the people around. But one boy on his own...? Jem picked up a big rock.

He clung to the rock through the long, dark hours, listening to the howling of the wolves.

At some stage, he drifted into a fitful sleep, the sounds of the night forming the backdrop to a horrible dream. In the nightmare, he was trying to run, but his legs wouldn't move. Something was coming up behind him, and coming up fast. It slammed a mighty paw upon his shoulder. The grizzly! It had him in its grip and was shaking him. Jem screamed out in terror, "Leave me alone! Leave me alone!" He awoke to find Swift Arrow's hand upon his shoulder.

U U U

Little Bear's father pulled Jem to his feet. His horse and the old grey mare stood side by side in the pale light of dawn. Without saying a word, Swift Arrow saddled the mare and hoisted Jem into the saddle.

They rode in silence for a long time before Jem could overcome his embarrassment and say anything.

"Thank you for coming to find me," he said to Swift Arrow.

"I didn't find you. You were not lost. I told your mother that you would know the way and catch up with us by daylight. But she was worried."

Swift Arrow actually believed that Jem could have found his way back on his own! Jem decided not to tell Swift Arrow how scared he had been.

They rode on across the prairie, with Tess trying her best to keep up with the long strides of Swift Arrow's horse. The horse was an Appaloosa, like Little Bear's. It had white spots like a sprinkling of snowflakes across its back.

"Little Bear says there are lots of Appaloosa horses in the valley where you live."

"Yes, there are many. Little Bear misses the horses. He misses the valley also. Sometimes he weeps at night for his home."

Jem was surprised. He couldn't imagine Little Bear crying. He always seemed so brave.

Lost on the Prairie

As they rode, Swift Arrow pointed out many things on the prairie that Jem had never noticed before. He showed Jem the rutted paths made in the earth by the buffalo herds as they moved down to drink from the wide waters of the North Platte River. He pointed out the wavering patterns that had been made in the sand by a passing rattlesnake, and the little mounds of earth piled high by prairie dogs.

At last, the white canopies of the wagon train came into sight up ahead. Before they reached the first few stragglers, Swift Arrow turned to Jem and asked, "What is it that frightens you as you sleep?"

Jem would have shrivelled up and died if anyone else had asked him that question, but somehow it didn't seem so bad coming from this gentle man.

"It's a bear. I have nightmares about a grizzly bear."

"You must make your peace with the bear, Jem," Swift Arrow said. "Look it in the eye and say, 'Bear, I am not frightened of you! Go away and don't come back until you can be friendly.'"

Jem doubted very much if that would work. Swift Arrow had not seen his bear. He had not looked into its angry red eyes or smelled its foul breath. But he promised Swift Arrow that he would try.

CHAPTER FOUR
THE BUFFALO HUNT

Day after day, the wagon train lumbered over the plains. The travellers felt as if the prairie would never cease rolling on ahead of them. The days dragged along with the dragging of their tired feet. The younger children amused themselves collecting wild flowers, playing games, and riding bareback on their ponies. The adults watched out for buffalo and other game. Fresh meat made a welcome change to an endless diet of salted bacon.

Whenever a herd of buffalo was spotted, it caused great excitement. Any man not in charge of an oxen team would grab his rifle and charge after the herd. The buffalo hunting wasn't always a great success though. Most of the men were farmers, not hunters, and they didn't have a lot of experience with guns.

Across the Oregon Trail

In fact, there had been several accidents already. One man had even shot off his own foot. Jem wished that he had a rifle, but he doubted he would be capable of hitting anything if he did – even his own foot.

Sometimes they saw large groups of Native Americans on the move. Their long lines of ponies trailed through the waving grass, dragging poles lashed to their sides. Hide was stretched between the poles into hammocks and carried tepees, skins, clothing, baskets full of utensils and food, and babies in their cradles. Dogs trotted alongside, some pulling small carts. Children ran and played among the group, or rode their shaggy ponies.

"Where do you think they're going?" Jem asked Little Bear.

"They're following the buffalo herds as they migrate."

"Do your people follow the herds, too?" Jem asked Little Bear.

"Our hunters come down to the plains to hunt the buffalo, but we do not follow the

The Buffalo Hunt

herds. We live mainly in the high country, where we hunt in the woods and fish in the rivers and streams."

One morning, they heard a noise that sounded like distant thunder. The noise grew louder and the oxen began to pull restlessly in their traces. On the horizon, they could see a massive black shape fanning out and coming towards them. From a distance, it looked as if the ground itself was moving like a black sea.

"Hold back your cattle!" yelled the captain. "Buffalo stampede!"

Jem had never seen or heard anything like it. There were so many buffalo thundering towards them that he couldn't have counted them if he had tried. The noise was deafening. Jem was sure the black mass of buffalo would run them down. At the last moment, they swerved and thundered off in another direction.

Quickly, the men grabbed their rifles and horses. Whooping and yahooing, they galloped off after the buffalo. Jem stood watching them with a mixture of envy and fear. He imagined what it would be like to fall off a horse and be trampled by thousands of hooves.

"Come and ride with me on Lightning," Little Bear called. He was mounted bareback. Grabbing Jem's hand, he pulled him up behind him. "Hang on and you'll be fine," he said.

Little Bear whirled Lightning around, and they galloped off after the others. Jem clung onto Little Bear with all his might. They were soon neck and neck with the vast herd. One huge bull was running on the outside. Little Bear cut him off from the rest. The bull pounded across the plains. Little Bear dropped the reins and pulled an arrow from his quiver. He fired the arrow and hit the bull in the chest. The bull thudded to the ground.

Little Bear pulled Lightning to a stop. Jem looked at the retreating buffalo and the riders whooping after them. "Quick, Little Bear. We can still catch up," he called out excitedly.

"You can only carry so much meat in your wagon," Little Bear said. "There is no need to kill any more."

The Buffalo Hunt

The family had fresh buffalo steaks for dinner that night. Little Bear showed Jem how to cook the buffalo meat and cut it into thin strips to dry. Before Jem went to bed, Ella whispered that he had been brave to go hunting with Little Bear.

Jem felt good as he fell asleep. Perhaps that was why he wasn't expecting the grizzly. It snuck up in his dreams, a huge beast the size of the buffalo Little Bear had killed. It lowered its shaggy head, as if it were about to spring on Jem and sink its claws into his neck. Jem was petrified. But then he thought of Swift Arrow's words. He looked the bear in the eye and said, "I am not frightened of you. Go away!" The huge bear growled at Jem, pawed at the air, then turned and shuffled away.

CHAPTER FIVE
FORT LARAMIE

The ground was sandier now, and strewn with rocks, so that the hooves of the oxen stirred up thick clouds of dust. The wagon train split into small groups to reduce the amount of dust thrown up into the faces of those following behind. Along the way, they passed by the strangest rocks that Jem had ever seen. Some looked like towering castles of gold. One jutted out of the ground like a gigantic finger pointing to the sky. The captain said it was called Chimney Rock.

At last, the tired, weather-beaten travellers reached Fort Laramie, a trading post and the gateway to the Rocky Mountains. They were now a third of the way to Oregon City. At Fort Laramie, they would have a much-needed rest for four days, carry out wagon repairs, and buy supplies before setting out on the steep ascent to the Rockies.

The fort was built of clay bricks dried yellow in the hot sun. The buildings formed a large square guarded by a wooden gateway and two-storeyed blockhouses. Most of the wagon party set up camp outside the fort, though some stayed inside. Jem envied those who were sitting on chairs and sleeping in beds.

He was fascinated by the people he saw. There were hunters and trappers from the mountains and Native Americans from many different tribes. The mountain men had weather-beaten faces, long straggly hair, and fringed buckskin clothes. They had all come to talk and to trade.

Jem overheard one trapper telling a yarn to the others. "It's so windy up there," he said, "that you could walk for ten minutes and end up two metres *behind* the place you started!"

Pack mules were tied up to the railings and loaded high with buffalo and beaver skins. The fort rang with the constant noise of hammering and the banging of blacksmiths' tools. A massive bearded man with a heavy accent was helping to repair a smashed wagon wheel. Another blacksmith was busy shoeing oxen with sturdy iron shoes, preparing for the rocky trail ahead.

Some of the wagon party made the decision to turn back at Fort Laramie. The trip had been tougher than they had expected, and they weren't prepared to go on. Secretly, Jem hoped his mother would come to the same decision. But, the night before, she had turned to Jem and said, "I know this trip has been hard on you since your father died, but he would have wanted us to go on. We can have a much better life in Oregon. Don't you worry, Jem. We'll be just fine."

Inside, Jem was screaming "No!", but he thought of his father and the dreams he'd had for the family. Although his father had been a skilled tradesman, he had found it hard to get regular work in the city. He had heard the stories about Oregon and life on the

Fort Laramie

New Frontier. Land was cheap and good for farming, and he dreamed of his family owning their own farm. He had spent their entire savings outfitting them for the trip.

"I can do it, Ma," Jem said, wondering how he was ever going to get them through the next two thousand kilometres.

Now they would have to buy in extra provisions for the journey ahead and get rid of some of the things they had no immediate need for. The oxen were struggling to pull the heavily loaded wagon over the tougher legs, and Jem's mother decided to trade in the few items of furniture they were carrying. She swapped their belongings for more salted bacon and biscuits.

The next morning, the Murphy boys told Jem about a trader they had found at the fort offering to barter luxuries, such as sugar, for goods. Jem found the trader selling supplies from the back of a wagon already loaded with barrels, baskets, books, clothes, furniture, and even a grandfather clock.

43

"Sir, would you consider trading some supplies for this jewellery box?" Jem asked the trader. "It's very old."

"Now, sonny, what would I do with a jewellery box way out here?"

Jem wondered the same about the clock, although he didn't say so.

"But seeing as how you're so polite," added the trader, "I'll give you a packet of sugar for it." Jem didn't think that sounded very good at all, but he had heard how expensive things were at the fort and knew he had very little choice.

That evening, around their campfire, they all looked forward to sugar in their tea. Ma put the pot on to boil, and Ella opened the packet of sugar. Jem stirred his tea and took a sip. It wasn't very sweet. He sipped some more and got a mouthful of grit.

"What's the matter, Greenhorn? Got grit between your teeth?" called Billy Murphy from the campfire alongside them. The Murphy boys collapsed into laughter.

Fort Laramie

Jem checked the packet of sugar. It had been mixed with sand. What a fool he'd been! Why had he trusted anything that the Murphys said? They loved to make him look stupid. They knew that the trader was a swindler.

When Jem went to the fort the following day, the trader and his wagon were gone.

CHAPTER SIX
HOLD YOUR FIRE!

They smelled them before they saw them. The hot breeze picked up the cloying smell of rotting carcasses and assailed the travellers. Up ahead, buzzards circled restlessly in the sky. Wolves, disturbed by the approaching wagon train, slunk off into the distance. It wasn't until the wagon train reached the river that Jem saw the mounds of buffalo carcasses spread like black pebbles over the valley floor.

The wagon train was ten days out of Fort Laramie and following the winding course of the North Platte River. Three days before, they had been overtaken by a band of heavily armed men. The men were impatient to pass without spending time to chat – unusual on the trail, where meeting others was a valued way of passing on information and news.

They had obviously had time to stop for some sport, however. The hundreds of buffalo they had killed hadn't been butchered for their meat, nor had they been skinned. The only things missing were their tails.

The captain rode among the carcasses, then returned to the wagons and yelled, "This won't look good for us. The Sioux will be angry if they see this slaughter." His words sent a ripple of fear through the wagon train. Since their journey began, many of the travellers had feared attacks from the Native Americans. But the captain had often reassured them that they were friendly. He told them of the times when Native Americans had helped to pull out stuck wagons or assisted in dangerous river crossings.

Jem spoke to Little Bear about it later. "Do you think we have anything to fear from the Sioux, Little Bear?"

"The buffalo are sacred to the native people, but the Sioux will already know who did this."

Early that afternoon, they reached a massive slab of rock that looked like a huge turtle lying in the middle of the plains. Travellers had nicknamed it Independence Rock, because wagon trains on the trail often made it to the rock in time for Independence Day. Jem and his party were a few weeks late, but they intended to celebrate anyway. Any thought of reprisals was forgotten as the party prepared for a dance that evening. Ma was even making a special pie from berries that Ella and Jem had picked along the trail.

Ella, Jem, and Little Bear rode the horses over to the rock and scrambled up its steep side. They climbed higher and higher, until they could see right across the valley down to the wagon train camped below. The rock was peppered with holes and crevices, and travellers had chiselled their names and messages into the granite. With a sharp stone, Ella chiselled her name in big letters: "ELLA WAS HERE! JULY, 1847."

Hold Your Fire!

It was Little Bear who first saw the riders approaching from the west. There were about seventy of them, riding fast and hard across the valley floor towards the camp. "Sioux!" Little Bear said. "We must warn the captain."

The three scrambled down the rock as quickly as they could without stumbling. Little Bear leaped onto Lightning and pulled Ella up behind him. Jem got onto Tess's back and yelled, "Go on ahead and tell the captain. I'll follow as fast as I can."

Jem reached the camp to find it in turmoil. The wagons had been drawn into a circle, and each tailgate was raised and locked into the wagon ahead to form a barrier. Men had grabbed their rifles and taken up positions beneath the wagons. The women and children were taking shelter behind the huge wagon wheels. Jem's mother saw him ride up and screamed for him to take cover. Behind him, Jem could hear the thunder of hooves. He dived off the horse and threw himself under the nearest wagon.

49

The captain was yelling instructions at the top of his voice. "Hold your fire! I repeat, hold your fire!"

Jem heard a rifle shot. At first he thought it was the Sioux firing, but then he realized they weren't even carrying guns. Then he saw one of the Murphy boys kneeling on the tailgate of a wagon. He was trying to reload his rifle to fire again. Before he got the chance, a man rode up at full gallop, leaned out from his pony, and snatched the rifle straight out of his hands. The Murphy boy was left on one knee with his hands up, frozen to the spot. Jem had never seen anyone look so surprised.

The rest of the Sioux group came cantering up and exchanged greetings with the captain. They had simply come to trade.

CHAPTER SEVEN
THE RIVER CROSSING

Wearily, the wagon train pushed on across the Oregon Trail, following in the footsteps of others who had gone before, in search of their dreams. Many hadn't made it. Some of the graves along the trail were marked with small wooden crosses; others had only a mound of stones to keep the hungry wolves at bay. Jem's mother always made a point of stopping and placing wild flowers on these grim reminders.

In one lonely spot, they came across a solitary wagon and its sad occupants. The mother and father were very ill – too weak to continue their journey. The wagon train with which they were travelling had been forced to go on without them. Their baby lay dead in the wagon, but they hadn't had the strength to bury her. Swift Arrow dug a grave for the little girl, and they left the couple with what medicine and comforts they could. As the wagon train pulled out, they all knew the couple wouldn't make it through the night.

In the early hours of one morning, Jem and his family were awakened by a massive crash of thunder. Lightning cracked open the heavens, and rain began to drive through the canvas of their tent. In seconds, their bedding and belongings were soaking.

"Grab what you can and head for the wagon," Ma cried. Outside, the camp was in chaos. As the lightning struck overhead, it lit up the whole valley. Jem could see other families struggling to lash down their tents and calm the frightened horses. He tightened the tent guys as best he could and ran to the shelter of the wagon. Ella and Ma sat huddled in a corner. Matthew was screaming as the thunder crashed above their heads.

The wagon train looked like a travelling clothesline as it pulled out the next day.

The River Crossing

Bedding, clothes, and sodden tents hung from the wagon hoops and flapped in the warm breeze. The oxen and wagons ploughed through a trail of thick mud. The wheels got stuck up to the axles, and several wagons had to be dug out of the brown ooze.

When they reached the banks of the Sweetwater River, they found its waters swollen by the overnight downpour.

"Our trail lies beyond the river. We have no choice but to cross," the captain shouted.

Swift Arrow rode out into the river to see where the safest crossing could be made and Jem's heart began to race. He wanted to yell out, "Turn back!"

In that instant, Jem was reminded of the day his father died. His father had been wading out into a wide river at the start of their journey when he had suddenly lost his footing. For some time, he had struggled in the swift current. The others told Jem that his father had quietly slipped beneath the water only moments before Jem had reached him.

"Everyone lead the teams out slowly and there should be no problems," Swift Arrow called out from the opposite bank.

Jem's mother touched him gently on the arm and said, "Come on. It will be fine." The leading teams clambered down the river bank and into the river. They were soon up to their chests in water that lapped at the wagons' running boards. Goliath seemed happy to follow, and the team headed down the bank. Jem led them into the water as Ella, Ma, and Matthew sat up on the front seat.

They were halfway across the river when Tess got loose from her tether and decided to swim away. Ella saw her and cried out, "Tess! Tess, come back!" Without thinking, she leaped off the wagon and into the water and began to swim after the horse. She was soon in trouble. Ella was not a good swimmer. The current was strong out among the eddies. She began to struggle and go under.

Fear gripped Jem until it nearly paralysed him. He hadn't been able to save his father;

The River Crossing

what if he couldn't save his sister? He dived out into the middle of the river and swam towards Ella. As he surged through the water, the same horrible thoughts went through his head. What if he failed again? What if Ella drowned before he could reach her?

After what seemed like an eternity, Ella's head bobbed into view and Jem dragged her out of the strong current. He pushed her up onto the river bank, where she lay in the mud trying to catch her breath. She was safe.

That night, Jem dreamed of the grizzly bear again. It came shuffling up to him with its awkward rolling gait. But, this time, Jem did not feel frightened. Instead, he reached out his hand to the bear. It stopped before him and took his hand gently in its huge mouth. It sat up on its haunches and playfully boxed Jem with one gigantic paw. The grizzly wanted to be friends.

CHAPTER EIGHT
ACROSS THE DESERT

Ever since they passed Independence Rock, the trail had gradually become an uphill climb. The wagon train laboured up steep ridges and across boulder-strewn river beds. The oxen struggled to pull the wagons up the rough tracks. It broke Jem's heart to see their feet cut and bleeding from the sharp stones. Goliath battled on, his strength and determination pulling the rest of the team through.

Jem and his mother agreed that they would have to try to lighten the load further if the oxen were to complete the journey. They tossed out any items that they didn't depend on for survival. Even things that they would need to set up their new home were discarded. Others in the train were forced to do the same. The trail was littered

Across the Desert

with pieces of furniture, luggage, blankets, clothing, wagon parts, tools, ploughs, and slabs of dried meat.

The travellers looked forward to reaching South Pass. There they would, at last, cross the Continental Divide and pass into Oregon country. They expected the pass to be dramatic, a narrow path through the Rocky Mountains walled by rocks hundreds of metres high. However, when they finally reached the pass, they found a broad, flat valley about thirty kilometres wide. Although they were now in Oregon country, they still had over sixteen hundred kilometres to go to their new home.

While they were camped, Little Bear showed Jem how to care for the oxen's torn knees and shattered hooves. They took the team down to the banks of a muddy stream and caked their legs in the thick black mud. "The mud can heal," explained Little Bear.

Back at camp, Little Bear heated some tar and painted it on the oxen's cracked hooves. It set solid, sealing the cracks. "This will help to strengthen their hooves. In about a week, we'll reach one of the toughest parts of the journey," he said.

Soon, as Little Bear had warned, the captain told them to prepare for a long trek across the desert. They filled containers with water and cut and collected grass for the animals. At sunrise, the wagons rumbled out onto a dry and featureless landscape. The desert stretched out before them, shimmering beneath a fierce sun.

For the first two days, the wagon train rattled across the hard ground during the heat of the day. The trail was so thick with dust that they couldn't see the wagon in front of them. Their clothes and faces were covered with a fine white powder. It filled their nostrils and coated their throats until it made them gag. The burning sun blistered their lips so badly that they had to rub axle grease on them to stop them from splitting. The wooden wagon wheels shrank in the dry air, and the iron rims that held the wheels together loosened. Some wheels rolled right off, and families were forced to stay behind to make repairs and to try to catch up with the rest of the group as best as they could.

Under the blazing sun, the oxen lowed with pain and fatigue. Even Goliath fell to his knees in the traces, his tongue lolling and eyes glazed. The water had to be rationed, and Jem felt like a traitor pulling the buckets away from the thirst-crazed oxen. Two of the Murphys' oxen lay down in their yokes and couldn't get up again. They were unyoked and left to die. All along the trail were the staring white skulls and sun-bleached bones of other animals that hadn't made it across the desert.

On the second evening, the captain called the group together and suggested they break camp at two o'clock in the morning and travel on in the dark. They could rest during the hot day, and travel on again through the cool of the night. Jem prepared the oxen for the early start. He tarred their shattered hooves and gave them some extra feed and as much water as could be spared. Ma tried to cook the family a decent meal from their meagre provisions. They were sick of the stale biscuits and dried, salted meat. Ella was getting irritable, and baby Matthew was crotchety, too. The last straw came for Ella when she climbed into her dusty bedding.

"Ma, Jem," she screamed out, "there's something in my bed!" Jem investigated and found a scorpion tangled in the sheet.

"I want to go home!" yelled Ella. "Why did you have to make us go on, Ma? Why didn't we turn back after Pa died?"

Ma didn't reply. For the first time, Jem noticed how pale, thin, and exhausted his mother looked.

They were woken in the early hours by the captain's booming voice calling them out of their beds. Ella and the other children held up lanterns to provide some light as the tents were packed up and the oxen harnessed. The wagon train set out into the black night, the

Across the Desert

children walking on ahead of the wagons and holding the lanterns high to light a path for the weary teams.

They travelled like this for the next two nights, resting as best as they could during the hottest part of the day. There wasn't a tree in sight, and no shade for the oxen and other animals. They were obliged to stand in the fierce sun, their heads hanging and breath coming in short, strangled bursts. The hot, dusty travellers slept beneath the wagons in the only shade they could find.

On the fifth day in the desert, Ella reached for the water barrel. "Ma, there's hardly any water left. We're going to run out! What can we do?" Ma looked at her with haunted eyes.

Then, on the seventh day, Jem and Ella found their mother lying unconscious under the wagon. They tried to wake her, but she lay lifeless in Jem's arms. Jem tried to think quickly. "Ella, get Swift Arrow. Run!"

Swift Arrow hurried back with Ella. "When did your mother last have water?" he asked.

"I'm not sure," Jem said, holding onto his mother's bloodless hand.

"I told her two days ago that the water was getting low," said Ella. "She must have stopped drinking to save it for us."

Swift Arrow took the canteen of water from around his neck, gently lifted their mother's head, and dribbled the water into her mouth. At first, she lay limply in his arms, then she choked and opened her eyes.

"Swift Arrow, what happened? Where are the children?"

"They're fine. But you need water and rest." He fed her some more water. She pushed the canteen away.

"This is your water. You'll need it."

"The children need your strength." He gave his canteen of water to Jem and walked away.

Before the wagon train set out again that evening, Jem made up a bed for his mother in the back of the wagon. Although it would be a rather uncomfortable trip, she was too weak to walk. Ella walked on ahead, carrying

Matthew in one arm and the lantern in the other, and Jem spurred the exhausted oxen after her.

The oxen had drunk the last of their water, and Jem didn't know how much longer they could go on. He asked the Murphys if they could spare a little water, as they had some in reserve since their two oxen died.

"Go ask your native friends. We ain't got any spare!" Old Man Murphy snapped at him. Everyone else faced the same problem – very little or no water. The were all praying for the end of the terrible desert.

In the dark of night, that end finally came. From up ahead came the excited cry, "Water! The oxen have found water!" Goliath tossed his head, and the team quickened their pace. Soon they joined the others at the edge of a shallow pond.

U U U

The next few weeks of the journey took them north-west towards the Snake River. They passed through a weird landscape punctured by craters, springs, and geysers. After the dry desert, it was heaven soaking in the warm waters of the springs and washing off the dust of the trail. Some springs tasted like soda water. One night, they camped at Steamboat Springs, near a beautiful geyser that made a whistling sound like the steamboats Jem had ridden on the Missouri River.

Their mother was still very weak, and the oxen thin and tired, when the wagon train rolled into Fort Hall. Like Fort Laramie, Fort Hall was a stockaded trading post. But it belonged to the British-owned Hudson's Bay Company, and the British flag fluttered from the blockhouse. The wagon train would stop here for a few nights to give the travellers time to replenish their supplies, rest the oxen, and fix their battered and broken wagons.

The British captain of the fort welcomed the guests, but tried to discourage them from travelling on. He told them stories of parties stuck on the difficult trails ahead, forced to abandon their wagons.

Jem's mother turned to Jem and asked uncertainly, "Do you think we should go on to Oregon?"

"Yes. We've made it this far. We must go on," Jem said, certain for the first time.

"Then you'll need this to trade for food and supplies," she said, handing Jem her wedding ring.

CHAPTER NINE
THE FALL

Jem traded his mother's gold ring for the supplies they would need for the rest of the journey. He also had the oxen reshod and repairs made to the wagon. The Murphys and some of the other families who had lost oxen were forced to have their wagons chopped down to half their size and refitted with only two wheels. This meant dumping even more of their load, leaving them only with food and water.

After resting for a few days, the wagon train was on its way again, its numbers greatly reduced from the original sixty or so wagons that had set out over four months ago. Now only forty wagons rattled along the trail, their boxes battered and canopies grey and torn.

The Fall

For many days, they followed the twisting course of the great Snake River. In some places, the river flowed through narrow canyons, and the oxen were forced to leave its side and haul the wagons up the surrounding hills. The travellers could see the surging waters below and hear the roar of many waterfalls.

Jem loved this land and the wild river that flowed through it. In the evenings, as they camped near the river, Little Bear showed him how to fish for trout. He made a long-handled shaft out of wood and carved a spear tip from bone. Once it was dark, they went down to the river with a torch to attract the trout. By its light, they fished from a jutting ledge of rock.

While they fished, Little Bear told Jem about the legend of Coyote and the creation of the Nez Perce. It was said that once Coyote fought a terrible monster who had swallowed all the fish and animals on the earth. Coyote cut out the monster's heart and told the fish and animals to leave through the opening. He then created the Native American tribes by scattering the monster's body across the land. He made the Nez Perce from the blood on his hands, sprinkled with water, saying that they would be few in number but very strong.

U U U

Late one afternoon, after the wagon train had been climbing uphill for most of the day, they reached a dead end. It was as if the path had dropped right off the mountainside.

"We'll have to lower the wagons and oxen down," said the captain. They were organized into groups to help lower each wagon and team down the steep slope, one at a time. Long ropes and chains were tied to the axles of the wagons, and trees were cut to use as chocks on the wheels.

The Murphys insisted that their team could get down the slope without the help of ropes and men to hold the wagon back. They tied a

The Fall

log to the back of their wagon to drag on the ground and act as a brake. "The hill is steeper lower down," warned Swift Arrow, who had ridden his horse down to check the path. "The log will not be enough to stop the wagon."

"We don't need your advice, Swift Arrow!" Old Man Murphy snapped, and the Murphys set off over the hill.

One by one, the wagons were lowered down the steep hill. It was a slow and back-breaking process. When it came to Jem's turn, he led the team down while Swift Arrow, the captain, and six other men held onto the ropes. Goliath's position was changed from the head of the team to the back. Because he was the strongest, he was the best brake for the wagon.

The chocked wheels slid and the wagon butted up against Goliath. The men fought to hold the wagon at a slow, steady pace by heaving on the ropes. As the path neared the bottom, it fell away sharply. The men strained on the ropes, but they couldn't stop the heavy wagon rocketing forward and slamming against the haunches of the oxen. Goliath took the full force, bracing himself against the wagon's weight. Blood trickled down his legs from where the wheels hit.

"Whatever you do, don't let them break into a run or we'll lose it," called the captain.

Jem spoke reassuringly to Goliath as he had learned to do. Goliath remained braced against the load, holding the wagon steady. Jem could see Ma and Ella staring nervously up at them from the bottom of the hill. It looked a long way down, but Jem knew they could make it. "Slowly, boy. That's it."

Goliath and the other oxen managed to keep their footing in the loose shingle, as the wagon slipped and slid down behind them. Gradually, the ground levelled out and they reached the bottom in safety.

The Murphys hadn't been so lucky.

CHAPTER TEN
INTO THE MOUNTAINS

The Murphys' wagon lay upturned in a ditch at the bottom of the hill, its contents spilled all around. Barrels of flour and sugar were shattered, trunks smashed, and bedding and clothes covered with dirt. A wagon wheel was splintered and the wagon box twisted and bent out of shape. One ox was stretched out on the ground, and the other hobbled around on three legs. Billy Murphy and Little Bear were kneeling alongside the fallen ox. Billy held its huge head in his lap.

"He's only winded," Little Bear told the downcast Billy. "But the other one will need a few days for the leg to heal. They won't be pulling any wagons for a while."

The rest of the Murphys were trying to right the wagon, but they were finding it impossible to shift, lying as it was in the bottom of the ditch. Jem unhitched Goliath and his team and led them over. He ran a chain from the axle of the wagon to the yokes of the oxen and, with the oxen pulling and the men pushing, they just managed to haul the Murphys' wagon out of the ditch.

The captain rode up and exchanged terse words with Old Man Murphy. "You're an idiot, Frank Murphy. This wagon train can't wait for you. We reach Fort Boise in two days, where we'll rest. If you can catch up with us there, well and good. If not, good luck to you."

"But one of our oxen is lame!"

"You should have thought of that before driving it over the hill!" replied the captain as he rode off.

Jem felt sorry for the Murphys. They could not hope to catch up with a lame ox pulling their wagon. And it would take them at least a day to repair the wagon before they could even get on the road. Jem decided to speak to his mother about lending them one of their

Into the Mountains

four oxen. It was only a few more days to the fort, and Goliath was so strong he could make up for the missing ox.

She smiled when he asked. "Yes, Jem, if you think we can still make it to Fort Boise."

The Murphys said very little when Jem handed over the ox. They had already begun work on their broken wagon when the wagon train pulled out. Goliath was now on his own at the head of Jem's team. He led the wagon across rolling hills and into Fort Boise.

The fort was another of the Hudson's Bay Company's strongholds, serving the beaver trappers of the region. There weren't many trappers left now as the beaver fur trade was on the decline. The huge beaver populations that once lived in the rivers of the Rockies had been almost hunted out. The trappers lived alone in the isolated mountains for most of the year, coming down from the mountains mainly to trade.

The trappers told them tales of the road ahead. Beyond the fort lay the Blue Mountains, where the trees stood over sixty metres tall. They said that some of the trails were so steep that you might think you were climbing to heaven. And beyond the Blue Mountains lay the Cascade Range, where the mountains were even higher!

Jem knew that the trappers wanted to frighten them. One thing they said worried everyone though – winter was coming early this year. The travellers had already begun to feel the crispness of the dawn and heard the honking of Canada geese as they passed high overhead on their migration south. Early winter snows could close the mountain passes and trap the wagon train as it tried to cross the mountains.

On the eve of their departure, a trapper spoke to the group about a short cut that the wagon train could take, chopping days off their journey. "That way, you'll be sure to beat the snows," he said.

Swift Arrow warned that the mountains were full of unpleasant surprises. What might seem to be quick and easy routes only led to dead-end canyons and impassable ridges. People on horseback might be able to get through, but not oxen hauling wagons.

Jem fell asleep thinking about Swift Arrow's stern warning. Suddenly, he was in a nightmare world of towering mountains and ghostly rivers. In the nightmare, he was clinging desperately to the side of a mountain. Below him was a sheer drop into nothingness. A wheedling voice was telling him, "Go on. It's the quickest way. Go on! Jump! Jump!" But from somewhere else came the urgent grunts and growls of the grizzly bear, trying to warn him. The bear was calling him back, back, back to consciousness.

U U U

Jem was on the lookout for the Murphys all the time they were at Fort Boise. He had almost given up hope of seeing them again when they finally straggled into the fort. Their worn, pale faces showed the first signs of relief that they had caught up with the rest of the group. Jem's ox was led over, and Old Man Murphy muttered a begrudging thank you. Billy didn't say a word.

Now that the wagon train was on the road again, there was a new sense of eagerness in the air. They only had about eight hundred kilometres left to go. The Blue Mountains and the Cascades still lay ahead of them, but they had already passed through nearly two and a half thousand kilometres of tough terrain.

At Farewell Bend, they said goodbye to their companion, the Snake River. Their trail lay to the north-west and the foothills of the Blue Mountains, while the Snake headed north-east. At windswept Flagstaff Hill, Jem caught his first glimpse of the treacherous Blue Mountains. He could see how they got their name. From a distance, they shimmered grey-blue in the afternoon sun, their tops iced in snow.

Into the Mountains

In the Grande Ronde, a beautiful green valley ringed by snowy mountain peaks, the wagon train stopped for the day and they prepared to cross the mountains ahead. Jem took time out from his chores to go riding with Little Bear. Lightning cantered along the valley floor, his head up and ears pricked. But Little Bear hung back on his horse, and Jem wondered if something was the matter.

Jem drew Lightning to a stop and waited for Little Bear to catch up. The two boys rode together in silence through the valley.

"The horses don't seem to want to race today. Do you think something's the matter?" Jem asked, breaking the silence at last.

"They want to go home. They know it's very close, just over those mountains." Little Bear nodded towards the north-east. "I would like to go home, too."

"Won't you be going home at the end of the trip?" Jem asked.

"My father says there is nothing there for us any longer."

"What about your family?"

"The people in the first wagon train my father guided across the mountains got a terrible illness. My father came home sick. Then people in our tribe got sick. My mother was the first to die. Many others followed."

"Do you not have any family left?" Jem almost whispered.

"I have some. But my father blames himself for my mother's death. And he thinks it is his fault people in our tribe got sick and died. He cannot face going home."

Little Bear spurred on his horse and galloped back to camp, leaving Lightning and Jem far behind.

CHAPTER ELEVEN
THE SHORT CUT

For several weeks, the wagon train passed over a land of low-slung mountain peaks and heavily wooded slopes. The air smelled of pine, and soft needles carpeted the trail. The children gathered wild berries and climbed the tall trees. They made slingshots and fired at imaginary bears in the forest.

One chilly mountain morning, the wagon train came to a fork in the trail. The main path headed up a steep hill; the other followed the meandering path of a river.

"This is the short cut the trapper told us about," called the captain. "We'll take the short cut and follow the river's path." Everyone was pleased – everyone, except for Swift Arrow.

"This is a trappers' trail," said Swift Arrow. "The trappers go into the mountains to hunt, and then they come out again. They do not pass through. There is no way to get through the mountains from here."

"Well, I'm the leader of this train, and I'm taking the short cut." The captain rode on. Everybody geed their oxen and followed the captain. Jem and his mother hesitated.

"We should listen to Swift Arrow. He knows the mountains," said Jem.

"But we can't leave the group," Ma said.

"Please, Ma. I had a dream about this. We shouldn't go this way."

"Jem, that was just a dream! We have to go with the others."

U U U

For several weeks, the trail followed the path of the river along a pleasant green valley. There was plenty of grass for the oxen along the river bank and shelter under the tall pines for the campers at night. Perhaps the captain

The Short Cut

and trapper had been right, thought Jem. This was the easiest part of the trip yet.

Very slowly, the valley began to narrow. The rocks crowded in on both sides, until they were leaning menacingly over the path. The travellers found themselves in a narrow cutting in the mountain. It was as if the mountain had been sliced open with a giant knife, and they were struggling along a deep wound. The crack was so narrow and the mountain so high that only a slit of sky could be seen above. It was dark and dank, and the rocks dripped with moisture. The river ran alongside them, no longer a thing of dancing blue beauty, but black and sullen. The oxen picked their way along the stony trail, the wagons scraping up against the sides of the wet rocks.

They followed the trail until darkness fell and what little light they had from above was extinguished completely. There was no room to stop and set up camp along the narrow trail. They would have to travel on through the night. Once again, the lanterns were lit and the children carried them high to light the way. They looked like a procession of fireflies crawling through a long dark tunnel.

It wasn't until daylight that the trail began to open up. The wagon party spilled out onto a narrow plain. Jem gazed up in dismay at the tallest mountains he had ever seen. From this distance, it didn't seem that there was any way out except straight up. They would have to climb now.

The short cut had taken them into an area that wasn't marked on their maps. The captain was convinced that they would join up with the main trail soon, so the wagon train pushed on westward. They had already lost several weeks, and to turn back now would eat up more valuable time. The wagon train rolled across the plain towards the western mountains and began the uphill climb.

The oxen toiled against their traces and hauled the wagons up the never-ending slopes. At one stage, the trail became so steep that it

The Short Cut

looked as if the oxen would fall backwards and onto the wagons.

"We need some big chunks of wood to drive beneath the wheels," Jem called out to Ma and Ella as he braced himself against the back of the wagon. Ma handed a piece of wood to Jem, and he drove it under the wheels to stop the wagon from sliding back.

Up ahead, Goliath threw himself into the hill and dragged the rest of the team and the wagon up with him. Many of the other teams couldn't make it up on their own. Oxen had to be unhitched and sent back down to help. Some wagons were hauled up by eight or more exhausted oxen.

Everyone remained huddled around their campfires long into the evenings. The nights were becoming colder, and the bedrolls were no longer warm enough. Jem thought about the blankets and warm clothes they had thrown out earlier to lighten the load. In the mornings, they looked nervously towards the sombre grey sky for the first signs of snow.

The snow could not have threatened at a worse possible time for Jem. The wagon train was inching its way along a narrow path carved into a mountainside. A vertical cliff was on one side and a sheer drop on the other. There was only enough room for the wagons to pass in single file. The oxen moved on ahead cautiously, hugging the cliff. They might have passed by safely if it hadn't been for the snow.

It fell without warning in sudden soft flurries. Soon it was driving in, and Jem had difficulty seeing ahead. Ella and Ma, holding Matthew, were walking behind the wagon, trying to keep warm and dry. The snow was building up in piles on the ground, and the path was becoming slippery and slushy as the wagons ahead pushed on.

Jem wasn't sure how it happened. The wheels must have slipped on a snowdrift and lost traction. The wagon slid up against the two back oxen and they lost their footing. Jem saw Goliath brace himself to steady the team,

The Short Cut

but it was too late. They were all pushed forward in the slippery snow. Jem watched in horror as Goliath and his teammate seemed to drop off the side of the mountain.

"No!" screamed Jem. "Goliath!" He ran to the side of the mountain and found Goliath and the other ox scrambling among the rocks at the top of the sheer drop. The two oxen behind were trying to regain their footing as the wagon rolled forward, threatening to topple them all off the mountain. Quickly, Jem grabbed some rocks and chocked the wheels. But he knew it wouldn't be enough to hold back the weight of Goliath and the other ox.

"Everything's gonna go!" yelled Old Man Murphy, whose wagon had been travelling behind Jem's. "Cut those two front oxen loose or you'll lose the lot!"

Jem knew he was right. He pulled out his knife and scrambled down to where the oxen were still struggling. His heart sank at the thought of sending Goliath crashing to the rocks below.

As he bent over to cut the traces, they suddenly tightened. The back oxen dug their heels in and started to pull away from the precipice. The wagon was being hauled back! Jem could hear the Murphy boys yelling, "Pull, come on you mangy brutes! Pull!" They had hitched their own oxen to the back of Jem's wagon and were hauling with all their might. Now Goliath and the other oxen were able to get a foothold on the rocks and clamber away from the cliff face. Within minutes, the wagon, Goliath, and the rest of the team were standing on firm ground.

Jem thanked the Murphy boys, but Billy just said, "Get your wagon out of the way, Greenhorn!" and gave a mighty grin.

CHAPTER TWELVE
THE ROCK OF THE BEAR

The wagon train continued its climb up mountain slopes now slippery with freshly fallen snow. The cold, tired travellers searched desperately for a pass through the mountains, but every trail they followed only took them higher and higher.

Jem couldn't get to sleep in the bitter cold. He lay in his bedroll listening to the troubled breathing of his mother and sister, and praying for sleep and the dreams it might bring. He needed to see the bear. He knew the grizzly was trying to tell him something. When the bear did come, however, it had a message that Jem could not understand.

In the dream, Jem was walking on a long white cloud. It was very beautiful but, with each step, Jem was sure he was going to slip right through. Then, just when it seemed he would drop to his death, the bear appeared. It wanted Jem to follow it. Jem took an uncertain step towards the grizzly, and the cloud began to harden beneath his feet. He was on solid ground again! Then the bear lay down and rested its great head between its paws. In front of Jem's very eyes, the grizzly turned into a massive black rock. Jem reached out and touched the rock. It was hard and cold. Jem woke with a start.

Later in the day, as the wagon train struggled up the mountain, Jem saw a black rock off to their right. There was something familiar about the dark shape against the white snow. Then he recognized it. It was the rock in his dream. It was the bear! Finally he understood the message he had been given. This was the way they had to go to safety – towards the rock!

Jem leaped onto Tess and rode up to join the captain and Swift Arrow at the head of the wagon train.

The Rock of the Bear

"Captain, I think we should go that way," Jem said, pointing to the bear rock, "towards that big black rock between the mountains."

"What makes you think that? A built-in compass?" the captain replied, laughing.

"I think there's a pass there."

"Then you've got better eyes than me, boy. Go on, get back to your oxen."

Jem turned to Swift Arrow. "Please listen to me, Swift Arrow. I'm sure there is a way through. The bear told me!"

Swift Arrow looked towards the outcrop of rocks. His eyes narrowed. "The boy could be right, Captain," he said. "There's no snow on the rocks. Wind could be funnelling down a pass there and melting the snow." But the captain had already ridden on ahead, his face set decisively.

The weather worsened as the day wore on. The snow was no longer powder-soft against their faces, but stung with the fury of a thousand hornets. Ma and Ella wrapped their warm shawls around their faces, and

Ma cradled Matthew in her arms as they battled up the hill.

The oxen floundered on in the deepening snow until exhaustion brought the wagon train to a complete stop. They would have to rest until the storm passed. The travellers sought shelter under some scrappy pines. They were forced to sleep in their wagons, as the thick snow on the ground prevented them pitching their tents. Ma, Ella, Matthew, and Jem lay side by side in their cramped wagon. Outside, a strong wind beat against the wagon canopy, howling eerily.

"Ma, do you think all those stories about the Donner Party were true?" Ella asked as they listened to the wind. They had all heard the passing travellers' tales about a wagon train trapped by snow in the mountains the winter before. The stories filtering through said that over half the men, women, and children had either starved or frozen to death. Some said the living had been forced to eat their dead companions in order to survive.

The Rock of the Bear

"You know how people exaggerate, Ella," Ma said, "and the Donner Party were going to California, not Oregon. Anyway, they were lost, and we're not lost."

Oh, yes we are, thought Jem, although he didn't say that. Ma knew they were lost, too, only she didn't want to worry Ella.

Jem had known all afternoon what he had to do. He waited until the dead of night, when Ma and Ella were fast asleep and the other wagons were quiet. He left his mother a note and sneaked out to saddle Tess. He was worried that the ageing horse couldn't make it through the snow, but he had to try.

Remembering his night on the prairie, Jem was prepared this time with a lantern, matches, clothing, and food. He was trying to load the pack saddle in the dark when he heard a noise – was it the guards? They would want to know what he was up to. Jem peered out into the dark and saw a ghostly white shape approaching. It was Lightning! Little Bear was riding him.

Wordlessly, Little Bear leant forward and pulled Jem up behind him. The two riders slipped quietly into the freezing, windy night.

Little Bear waited until they were out of earshot to say, "My father told me what you saw today. I knew you would go back to the rock."

U U U

The wind whipped up the mountainside and hurled snow in the boys' faces as they clung to Lightning's back. Jem carried the lantern until the wind snatched it out of his hands and they rode on in the darkness. They couldn't see a thing in front of them; all they knew was that they had to keep heading straight down the mountain to retrace the wagon train's path.

Lightning was brave and surefooted. He stepped out into the blackness and picked his way down the mountainside with care. Jem felt as if they were walking off the face of the Earth into a freezing black void. The cold wind cut through their flesh and chilled their bones.

Slowly, they fought their way through the long cold night. Jem and Little Bear took turns riding in front, so that the back rider got some shelter from the blasting wind. At some stage, the snow stopped falling, but the cold wind wouldn't give up its attack, hurling itself against them like an invisible battering ram. It was Lightning who was hit with its full force, but he only slowed if he sensed the boys slipping from his back.

At last, a cold, pale dawn rose to greet the tired riders. Jem peered through the growing light for any sign of the black rock. "There it is. There's the bear!" he finally cried, pointing along the mountainside.

"You're right. It does look like a bear!" Little Bear called back above the wind. "It's crouching between the mountains with its long snout between its paws. It looks as if it's about to leap off the mountain!"

Before setting off towards the rock, Jem tied a bright ribbon from Lightning's saddle blanket to a tree, so that they would know the way back to camp. As they got closer to the huge rock, they could see that the front legs of the bear straddled two slopes. The bear was crouching over a narrow path between the mountains. "You were right, Jem. The bear is guarding a pass!"

The boys followed the pass a little way into the mountains. It showed no signs of ending. Instead, it gradually widened, gently pushing the mountains aside.

"We have to ride back and tell the others, Little Bear. The wagon train can easily get through here." Jem's excitement was infectious and the two boys started to laugh.

CHAPTER THIRTEEN
THE WAY HOME

Jem and Little Bear retraced their path until they found Lightning's ribbon tied to the tree. Then they began the long uphill climb back to camp. They were so excited with their news that the cold no longer mattered. The wind had dropped, and sunlight pushed its way feebly through the clouds. Lightning's step was light and quick, and it wasn't long before the camp emerged out of the snow.

Jem's mother ran to his side and gave him a hug. "Swift Arrow knew that you would make it back," she cried with relief.

"Ma, we've found a pass through the mountains. We have to tell the captain!"

But, when Jem found the captain, he was not interested. "Go back to your wagon and get ready to pull out, boy. We don't have time to listen to your crazy dreams." He mounted his horse and prepared to ride off.

"But we saw the pass!" cried Jem, grabbing the reins. "It leads through the mountains!"

"Let go of my horse," the captain bellowed. Then he turned to Swift Arrow. "Take this boy back to his mother, Swift Arrow, before I lose my temper."

"We should listen to him, Captain. At least go back and check his story."

By that time, some of the others in the wagon train had overheard the argument.

"What's this about some pass, Captain?" Old Man Murphy called out.

"The boy has some crazy notion about a way through the mountains back there. It looked like a pile of rocks to me."

"We've seen it!" Jem insisted.

"It probably goes for five hundred metres and then pulls up short against a cliff face. I say we have to go on," the captain said.

"Yeah, and what does Swift Arrow say?" Old Man Murphy asked.

The Way Home

"We should go back," Swift Arrow replied.

"Well, I'm following Swift Arrow," Old Man Murphy announced to those gathered around.

With that, the others turned back to their wagons and prepared to follow the Murphys' lead. The captain looked levelly at Swift Arrow and, without any trace of bitterness, said, "Swift Arrow, it looks as if the boy has won. I don't know why you are so convinced he's right, but let's go and find out if he is."

U U U

"Thank you for believing in me, Swift Arrow," Jem said when Swift Arrow rode up alongside their wagon.

Swift Arrow pulled up his horse and looked down at Jem. "You were brave to make your peace with the bear. You are worthy of belief."

"Why can't you make your own peace, Swift Arrow? Why can't you go home?" Jem asked. Swift Arrow didn't reply. He just stared ahead of him into the distance as if he hadn't heard a word.

The wagon train travelled on for two days along the mountain pass. Sometimes Jem wondered if they would indeed come to a dead end, but he trusted in the bear. It had not been back to visit him in his dreams, and Jem knew he would never see it again.

On the afternoon of the second day, the captain called out from the head of the wagon train, "Mount Hood, I can see Mount Hood!" Jem urged Goliath and the team on, and the pass began to widen out ahead of them. As they turned a bend, the snow-capped cone of Mount Hood rose up to greet them.

"Below Mount Hood is Willamette Valley," Swift Arrow explained to Jem, Ma, and Ella. "You are nearly home."

CHAPTER FOURTEEN
JOURNEY'S END

They only had a few more weeks of travel ahead of them. Everyone was excitedly making plans for when they arrived in Willamette Valley. Some of the travellers would go on to Oregon City, but most planned to settle in the fertile valley that they had all heard so much about.

Jem, Ma, and Ella talked about the land they would buy and the first home that they could truly call their very own. They playfully argued about what they would farm. Ma wanted to grow apples, so that she could see them blossom in the springtime, Ella wanted to breed horses, and Jem wanted to farm the cattle he had come to love, thanks to Goliath. Secretly, he also dreamed of breeding horses as quick and clever as Lightning. He would miss Lightning when the journey was over, but he would miss his new friend, Little Bear, even more.

Little Bear was very quiet when they talked about their new home. Jem knew it was because he was thinking about his own home and family. He wondered where Swift Arrow and Little Bear would go now that the journey was nearly over. Swift Arrow would probably guide yet another group of migrants along the long and dangerous trail. It was not much of a life for Little Bear.

Early one morning, as Jem was harnessing the oxen, Little Bear came up leading the horses. His father's horse was packed high with gear, and Jem realized that the time had come to say goodbye. He felt a sharp pang of sadness.

"I've come to say thank you," Little Bear said to Jem. "My father told me this morning that we are going home. He said that you spoke to him, and it touched his heart. Because of you, I will see my family again."

Journey's End

Little Bear took Lightning's reins and handed them over to Jem. "He belongs with you. You have both been brave, good friends."

Before Jem could say anything, Little Bear turned and walked away.

FROM THE AUTHOR

I love reading about great journeys. Part of me would love to saddle up my horse and start out on some great overland trek of my own. I doubt, however, that I would have had the courage to follow the Oregon Trail. In researching this book, I read lots of diaries written by those who made the journey. They were very brave people. It was a long, tough journey across a wild and lonely land. But the things they saw! Imagine a prairie covered with buffalo as far as the eye could see, or a vast desert bathed in a blood-red setting sun.

In parts of the United States today, you can still see the deep ruts cut in the ground by the wagon wheels as pioneers followed the Oregon Trail. Perhaps, one day, I will just saddle up and follow those tracks, and see where the spirit takes me.

Susan Brocker

DISCUSSION STARTERS

1. Jem and his family travel a great distance to find a better life for themselves. Have you ever had to travel to a new place? If not, where do you think your family would have more opportunity, and what hardships can you imagine might come with that?

2. When two of the Murphys' oxen die and one becomes lame, Jem lends them one of his family's oxen. Why do you think he made this sacrifice? Have you ever sacrificed something for another person? What was the situation?

3. Discuss the ways this story relates to the saying, "The grass is always greener on the other side." Do you think this saying applies to this story? Why/Why not?